Chanukah in Chelm

Chanukah

David A. Adler ◆ Kevin O'Malley

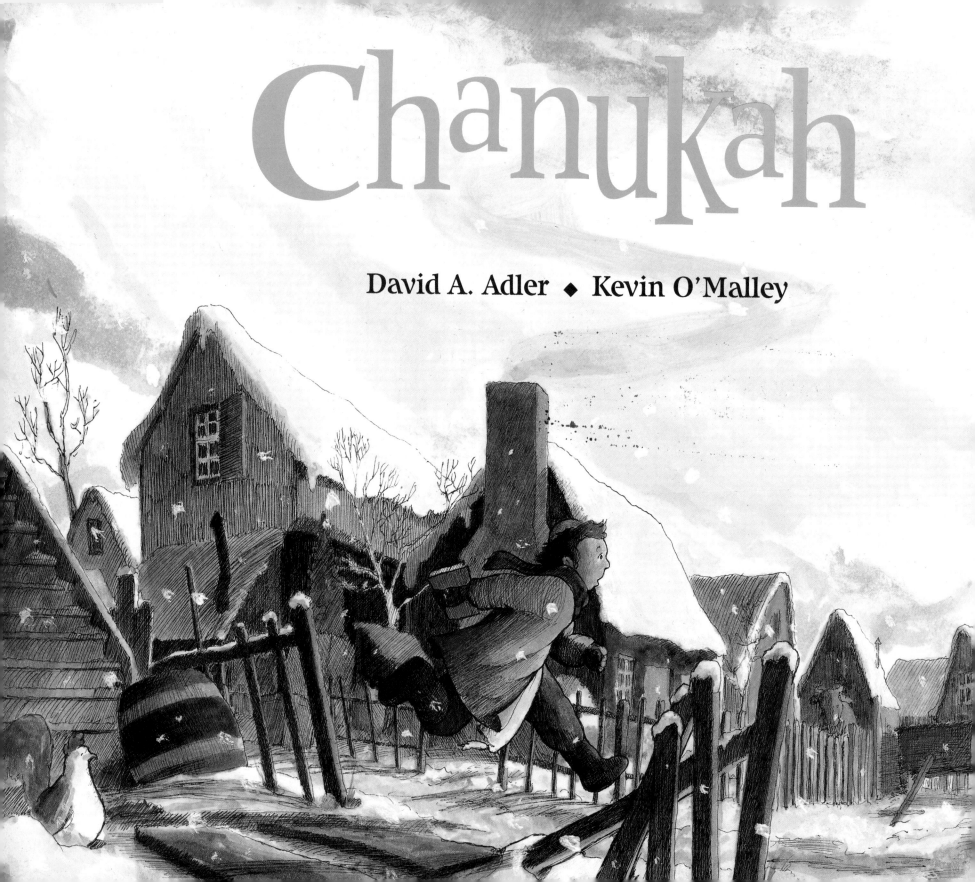

in Chelm

Lothrop, Lee & Shepard Books ◆ Morrow

New York

for my cousins, Irad and Itai
— D.A.A.

for all my Jewish relatives
— K.O.

Oil wash on pen and ink was used for the full-color illustrations. The text type is 14-point Isbell.

Text copyright © 1997 by David A. Adler
Illustrations copyright © 1997 by Kevin O'Malley

Published by Lothrop, Lee & Shepard Books
an imprint of Morrow Junior Books
a division of William Morrow and Company, Inc.
1350 Avenue of the Americas, New York, NY 10019

Printed in Hong Kong by South China Printing Company (1988) Ltd.

2 3 4 5 6 7 8 9 10

Library of Congress Cataloging-in-Publication Data
Adler, David A.
Chanukah in Chelm/by David A. Adler; illustrated by Kevin O'Malley.
p. cm.
Summary: When the rabbi tells Mendel to get a table for the Chanukah menorah,
Mendel makes the task more difficult than it should be.
ISBN 0-688-09952-1 (trade)—ISBN 0-688-09953-X (library)
[1. Jews—Poland—Folklore.   2. Folklore—Poland.   3. Chelm (Chelm, Poland)—Folklore.]
I. O'Malley, Kevin, ill.   II. Title.   PZ8.1.A23Ch 1997   398.2'089'924—dc21   [E]   96-53127   CIP AC

about Chelm and Chanukah

There are two Chelms. One is a real town in Poland. Jews lived, studied, and prayed there for hundreds of years. They suffered there, too, from poverty and prejudice.

The other Chelm, the one in this story, is a town famous in Jewish folklore. Its people had good hearts, great dreams, but very little sense. They suffered, too—from their own foolishness.

The people in both Chelms celebrated Chanukah, the eight-day holiday that begins each year on the twenty-fifth day of the Hebrew month of Kislev (November/December). With lights, foods prepared in oil, games of dreidel (a four-sided spinning top), and gifts, the holiday celebrates the victory of a small band of fighters over a king's huge army in a struggle for religious freedom. It celebrates, too, the small jar of pure oil, enough to burn in the ancient Temple in Jerusalem for just one day. The oil miraculously burned for eight days, until more could be prepared.

Moshe, what should a man know before trying to teach a dog?

Mendel was the caretaker of the Chelm synagogue. Early each weekday morning, he readied it for services. He swept the floor and straightened the benches and prayer books. He opened the doors and greeted everyone who came to pray.

After services, people left for their homes and for work. Mendel closed the synagogue doors. Then he gave Rabbi Nachman a breakfast of herring in cream sauce, a warm roll, and a cup of hot tea.

No, Lysar, I would never talk with my animals, even if they said please.

More than the dog. Right, Spot?

One winter morning, as Mendel was pouring the tea, the rabbi said, "Don't forget, after you put away the prayer books, set the menorah by the window. Tonight is the first night of Chanukah."

Rabbi Nachman dipped his roll in cream sauce, and Mendel went to the storage closet. On a small table there, he found the menorah, a jar of oil, and a few wicks left from the previous Chanukah. He took the menorah, oil, and wicks and put them on the floor by the window.

"Mendel, you'll need a table," the rabbi said, "for we are commanded to set our lights where others can see them and be reminded of the Chanukah miracles."

Mendel looked at the menorah. The rabbi was right. Without a table, it couldn't be seen through the window. It could hardly be seen in the synagogue.

Mendel went to the closet again. He looked under the table and over it. He even moved the table aside so he could look behind it. But he couldn't find a table to place by the window.

Rabbi Nachman was studying the holy books. Mendel didn't want to disturb him, so he stood by and waited.

After a long while the rabbi looked up.

"Is it time for lunch?" he asked.

"No, Rabbi," said Mendel. "It's the table. I've looked everywhere, and I can't find it."

"So you didn't find the table," the rabbi said. "Well, we can't leave the menorah on the floor. Go see Berel the carpenter. Maybe he can loan us a table for Chanukah. And hurry back. We need it by nightfall."

Mendel put on his coat and left the synagogue. He walked through the forest to Berel's workshop. When he got there, Berel was looking at a ladder he had just finished building.

"I'm confused," Berel said. "I walked away for a moment, and now I don't remember which end of the ladder is the top and which is the bottom."

Mendel shrugged his shoulders. He didn't know either.

"It's a big problem," Berel said. "If I set the ladder against the apple tree and the ladder is upside down, then when I think I'm climbing up the ladder, I'll really be climbing down. And when I think I'm going down, I'll really be going up."

"But why are you climbing an apple tree?" Mendel asked. "There are no apples on it now. It's winter."

"Maybe you're right," Berel said. "Maybe it *is* winter."

"Of course it is," Mendel said. "And that's why I'm here. Tonight is the first night of Chanukah. The rabbi needs to borrow a table, so the menorah can be seen through the synagogue window."

"A table?" Berel asked.

"Yes, a table," Mendel told him, "with legs and a flat top for the menorah."

"Ah, a table," Berel said. "Come with me."

SALE!
TWO-
LEGGED
TABLES

He took Mendel into the workshop and pointed to a large wood table by the window. "This table has four sturdy legs and a solid top," Berel said. "See how strong it is!" And he jumped on the table and began to dance.

Mendel looked at the table. He tried to imagine it with a silver menorah on top instead of a dancing Berel. Then he looked through the window and noticed it was getting dark outside. The sun would be setting soon.

"The table is just right," Mendel said. "I must hurry if I'm to get it to the synagogue by nightfall."

Berel tied the table to Mendel's back and led him to the door.

He's all-shtetl champ.

What a good dancer!

The table was heavy. Mendel walked slowly through the forest. At times he had to bend over so that the table's legs wouldn't hit a low branch. After a while, Mendel had to rest. His legs ached from carrying the heavy table. So he untied it and sat beneath a tree.

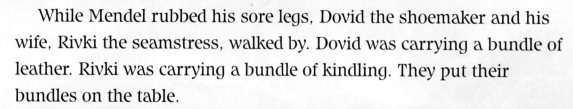

While Mendel rubbed his sore legs, Dovid the shoemaker and his wife, Rivki the seamstress, walked by. Dovid was carrying a bundle of leather. Rivki was carrying a bundle of kindling. They put their bundles on the table.

They told Mendel, "We're tired of carrying these."

Mendel told Dovid and Rivki, "I'm tired of carrying the table."

"Well," said Rivki, "if your table will carry our bundles, we'll help you carry your table."

Mendel picked up one side of the table. Dovid and Rivki picked up the other side of the table. They quickly dropped it.

"The table with our bundles on it is too heavy to carry," Rivki said.

How many Chelmites does it take to move a table?
One to hold the table and ten to move the earth.

Dovid bent and looked under the table. Mendel and Rivki bent and looked at Dovid.

Dovid told the table, "You have four strong legs. If we can walk to the synagogue on two legs, surely you can walk on four."

Dovid grabbed his bundle of leather. Rivki grabbed her bundle of kindling. They started to walk away.

Mendel tapped on the table to get its attention. "Follow us," he told the table. Then he ran to catch up with Dovid and Rivki.

Without the table, Mendel was able to walk quickly. He reached the synagogue just before nightfall. He sat on the front steps of the synagogue and waited for the table.

Here table, table. Come on, boy!

Mendel greeted the people who arrived for evening services. He wanted to greet the table, too, to show it where to stand, right by the window. But the table never came.

"Where's the table?" Rabbi Nachman asked.

"It was a strong table," Mendel told the rabbi, "but it was stupid. It got lost in the forest."

"Well, come inside," the rabbi said. "It's time for evening services."

After the prayers, Rabbi Nachman told Mendel, "It's time to light the menorah. Without a table, people outside won't see the lights, but *we'll* see them. Please get me a match."

I've been saving the sun I caught this summer for the first night of Chanukah!

How did you break your arm?

I fell out of the tree while I was raking leaves.

Mendel went to the storage closet. The box of matches was on the small table. As soon as Mendel picked up the box, he noticed the table under it.

"See how foolish I am," Mendel said to the table. "I was waiting outside for you, and all this time you were here, waiting for me. You must know a shortcut through the forest. I shouldn't have told you to follow me. I should have followed you.

"Come," Mendel continued. "You have to go to the window." The table didn't move. "You must be tired from all the walking," Mendel said. "But I'm not. I'll carry you."

He carried the table into the synagogue and set it by the window.

Rabbi Nachman spoke about the Chanukah miracles—about the small band of fighters who beat the king's army and about the oil that kept burning. He said the blessings and lit the Chanukah lights. Then he wished everyone a happy holiday.

The people of Chelm went to their homes to light their own menorahs. Rabbi Nachman opened his holy books and studied. And Mendel sat by the window and watched the lights burn. When they went out, he wished the table a happy Chanukah and went to prepare the rabbi's dinner.